STUFFIE HOSPITAL LONDON: COLLECTION 1

ELLIE ROSE

CONTENT NOTES

A London Little's Llama: Please be aware that this story has a children's hospital as a setting. It also references a sibling's death during childhood (off page, and way before the events of book).

A London Little's Moo: Please be aware that this story has references to a mean previous Daddy (off page, and his actions always acknowledged as bad). As a result of that relationship, Tillie has some trauma that manifests as anxiety, and has a panic attack on page.

A London Little's Dragon: Please be aware that this story references previous toxic relationships (off page, and before the events of book).

I hope that I have treated these experiences and emotions with the care that they and you deserve.

For the Lilo to my Stitch; thank you for being my person.

STUFFIE HOSPITAL

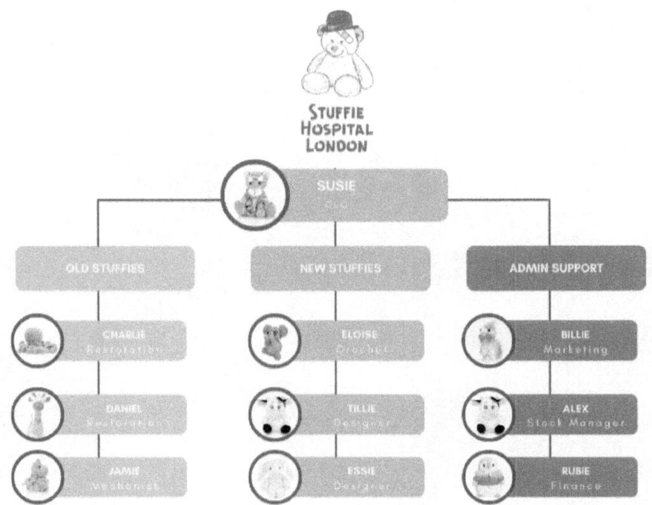

A LONDON LITTLE'S LLAMA

A London Little's LLAMA

ELLIE ROSE

❧   I   ❧

Looking up at a sign that read *Llama's Ward*, Billie Harrington gulped. She'd thought she'd have at least a week to settle into her new job, but she'd been pulled aside by Susie Jenkins that morning as she'd arrived, and taken straight up to the CEO's office.

"You see Billie," Susie had said, all smiles, "this project has only just been greenlit by the hospital board – the medical hospital, that is, not Stuffie Hospital London's – and we want to prove to them that they've made the right decision coming to us."

Billie had nodded. She'd known all about the upcoming project, and her ideas for how to make it a success had been part of the reason they'd offered her the job in the first place, but she hadn't even had a day to settle and they were sending her out into the world on her own, to showcase what she could do?

Luckily, that hadn't quite been true. One of Stuffie Hospital London's designers, Tillie, and the mechanics specialist Jamie, had been assigned to the project, and they'd introduced themselves in the car over.

Even so, she hadn't expected to be *here* on her first day.

The Caring Bears Project was a charity endeavour that had been set up in the US branch of Stuffie Hospital, but it had taken a while before its British counterpart had managed to persuade a children's hospital that it would be of use. The idea was that stuffies could be operated on, before children's operations, to help alleviate fears, or be given haircuts and scars and prosthetic limbs, so that a child could have a bear who looked like them.

It was one of the things that had drawn Billie to apply for the marketing role in the first place. Yes, she'd get to do normal marketing work, but she also got to do this, got to bring some cosy joy to children who needed it the most, and raise awareness for the children's hospital's work at the same time.

"You coming Billie?" Tillie asked over her shoulder.

Billie nodded, shifted the bag of bears in her arms and followed the other woman through the door into a riot of colour.

The walls were painted with bright colours, and everything from polka dots to stripes to a mural of beloved cartoon animals decorated them.

They made their way into the playroom, and Tillie and Jamie started setting out the stuffies in a line. Billie set down her bag of bears and wandered over to the bookcase, taking a peek at some of the books. That had been her favourite part of the hospital playroom when she'd visited her sister as a kid. Everyone else had always fluttered around Sammie, and Sammie had performed for them, putting on plays and singing and dancing. Billie hadn't liked to draw attention away from her sister, and also, bluntly, hadn't wanted any of it for herself. She'd always been perfectly content to sit in the corner of the playroom with a book, and let the world float right on by her.

Her family had been perplexed, then, by her decision to go into marketing as an adult, but it wasn't nearly as client-facing as most people thought. She'd work with a few key stakeholders, and spend a lot of time on her computer, organising photoshoots remotely and running social media campaigns from her desk. All that reading had finally paid off.

But for this job though... For this campaign she'd go to the ends of the earth and back.

She turned towards the others, and snapped some pictures of Tillie and Jamie, setting up the table of stuffies. There were about thirty bears, and each child would get to pick one for their very own. Tillie would help them rework and design customisation, and Jamie would help make it come to life.

And Billie would catalogue it, whilst making sure to keep the children out of the footage. All the parents had signed release forms, but she had seen first-hand the impact that cameras had on Sammie, the forced smiles and the exhaustion it brought with it, so most of what she was doing would focus on the team and on the teddies.

She was in the middle of taking a photo of a particularly cheerful rainbow bear, when a loud and rather irate voice came from behind. "What on *earth* do you think you're doing?!"

Turning round, she met dark brown eyes and blinked rapidly. The man before her wore a surgeon's green scrubs, and looked as cross as anyone she'd ever seen. "Hello, I'm taking photos for..."

"No photos."

"But..."

"No *damn* photos!" The surgeon's voice had dropped to a fierce whisper, and the words were forced out through his teeth. "These are children and they are not to be photographed or otherwise taken advantage of."

"Please, doctor, we would never…"

"No," his voice cut across hers and she almost took a step backwards. "These children are under my care, my protection, and they should not be exposed to *marketing types*," he spat those last words, "who plan to capitalise on their illness."

Billie felt her hands tremble, but she raised her chin and met his gaze head on. "Excuse me, but I think you have this project mistaken. We are here to provide bears for the children. There will be no photographs of the children taken."

"Then tell me why the parents have signed release forms."

"Because we will be talking to them, and we may use snippets of conversation in this campaign to raise awareness *for the hospital*." She emphasised the final words in the sentence, and felt a sigh of relief when his shoulders dropped, and he took a step back. "The photoshoot will focus entirely on before and after photos of the bears, which have been donated. As has my time and the time of my colleagues."

"Ah."

"Yes. So, if you don't mind, doctor, I'd like to get back to my work?"

She thought he'd leave then, embarrassed by his mistake, but he didn't, instead following her round the room.

"I've dealt with too many piranhas to leave things to chance. I hope you understand Ms…?"

"Harrington. Billie Harrington."

He extended a hand, "Mark Taylor."

Billie looked at the surgeon's hand and then shook it tentatively. "I'd best be getting on with my work now please, Doctor Taylor."

"Of course, Ms Harrington."

And then he really did leave, brushing his hand over the back of his shorn head. Looking at his retreating figure made her feel all weird and jumbly inside; there'd been something reassuring about his presence, and a traitorous voice at the back of her head made her realise that she wouldn't have minded him using that stern voice on her outside the hospital.

❧ 2 ❧

The following day, Billie went straight to the Llama Ward in the morning. Tillie and Jamie were going away to work on the designs for the chosen bears, but she wanted to get to know the staff and children a little better.

Stepping through the doors, this time she let it really hit her.

Hospital wards had a feel to them. Something that was almost tangible. And that went doubly for children's wards. There was something about the space that made it feel weirdly joyful and grief-stricken, as if everyone in the space was one moment away from crying.

Everyone except the nurses.

She stopped off at the nurses' station, and handed over a big box of chocolates, and some tiny bears that she'd gotten sign off from Susie to bring. "For the team," she said, smiling through her anxiety.

"Billie? Billie Harrington?" A familiar voice cut through the background noise, and Billie turned and found herself swept up in a warmly recognisable hug. "I have not seen you in many years; look how grown you are!"

Sade Okoro had been Sammie's favourite nurse, and it felt jarring to see her here, in a children's ward, without her sister chattering away in the background.

"What brings you to my ward?"

"Your ward?"

The older woman gestured around, "Matron of Llama Ward."

Billie smiled then; the first genuine smile she'd felt grace her face for some time. "I can't think of a better Matron. And I'm here with Stuffie Hospital London; I'm coordinating the campaign with the bears?"

Matron gave out a peal of laughter. "Oh, please tell me that it was you who put Mark Taylor in his place!"

A quiet chuckle. "I'm sure Doctor Taylor didn't mean to be rude."

"I certainly didn't."

Billie spun on the spot and flushed scarlet when she saw the handsome surgeon looking ruefully at her. "I mean… I…"

"I think," said a small voice from close to the floor, "That he probably deserved it."

Doctor Taylor pulled a face at the little girl standing next to Billie, and the girl giggled. "I probably did. How do you think I should make it up to her, Kafia?"

"Cake!" The word was met with rally of cries and soon there were a group of children, all watching them eagerly, awaiting the cake that Billie wasn't entirely certain that they'd promised anyone.

"Well, if we're going to get some cake," she cast a glance at Matron Okoro, who rolled her eyes and nodded, "Then what type should it be?"

Once all the votes had been tallied, and the only vote that really mattered (Matron's) noted down, Doctor Taylor headed off to procure some immediately. He'd been planning on bringing it in the following day, she could tell, but the children had insisted. Just as they insisted that she follow them into the playroom, and read them story after story.

It felt weirdly comforting, doing something that she did at home to soothe herself, here, in this place, to soothe these children.

The older children held back, of course, too old for tales of dancing pandas and naughty bunnies, but they fell upon the cake that Doctor Taylor returned with, with as much aplomb as the rest of them.

"Just you today?" he asked, when the ward was alive with the sound of cake consumption.

"Yes," Billie smiled shyly. "The rest of the team are back at Stuffie Hospital. They'll be here later this week. I just wanted to come and make sure that I knew where I wanted to take the photos of the made-over bears. And drop something off for the nurses; projects like this are great, but they cause chaos."

He nodded at that. "And often leave more stress in their wake, no matter how much good they do, or money they raise."

"I know, hence the thank you gift to the nursing team."

Doctor Taylor looked at her thoughtfully. "You've been here before; that's how Sade knew you."

"I..." her words were robbed from her, hijacked by memories. "Yes. My sister was on this ward. But that was a long time ago."

So many years ago. This was the first time she'd been back, and it felt surreal to walk down the hospital corridors without her stuffie in hand; the llama stuffie going with her to visit the Llama Ward.

He looked as though he didn't know whether to ask a question or not.

The question.

The one that everyone asked when they found out about Sammie.

"No," she said, unprompted. "She didn't get better." And then she took another bite of cake, because nothing made the loss of Sammie better, and treating it as matter-of-fact sometimes meant people didn't offer meaningless platitudes.

"I'm sorry."

"That's okay," Billie said, even though it kind of wasn't. "It's why I wanted to be a part of this project." She stood, "Thank you for the cake, Doctor Taylor."

"Mark, please call me Mark."

"Mark."

His eyes were kind and Billie realised that if she didn't step away from him soon, she was going to burst into tears, and where would that leave them?

T hat Wednesday was her third day working for Stuffie Hospital London, and the first that she actually got to spend in the office.

She shared it with Rubie, a sweet trans woman whose bubbly personality seemed at odds with her role as finance manager, at least until she saw the other woman handle some contractors who were threatening to charge way too much for repairs. But she was super friendly, and seemed determined to take Billie under her slightly chaotic wing.

"I blame the ADHD," said Rubie with a grin. "You spend four years waiting for a diagnosis, and in the meantime, it turns you into a chaos gremlin. I'm great at my job though. Numbers are one of my special interests, so the day-to-day spreadsheeting is my idea of heaven!" And she proved her point by almost forgetting lunch because she was so ensconced in her work.

It was nice to finally settle into her space. The Stuffie Hospital London site was small, much smaller than its American counterpart because, as Susie liked to point out, in a country forty times smaller, you have forty times less space.

It was in an old house in London, with the upstairs split into the business office (where Billie was based), Susie's office, and the designers' office; and the downstairs was workshop and warehouse in one. There was a staffroom in the conservatory at the back, just past the kitchen.

"Susie wanted to go cosy," explained Rubie, when they stopped for lunch. "We're a smaller operation, but we're good at what we do and have enough celebrity clients to be able to do projects like Caring Bears. How're you finding it?"

Billie, bemused at the speed of which these words had rattled out of Rubie's mouth, grinned. "It's nice. I'm glad I'm doing something to help."

Just then Jamie popped his head around the door of the conservatory. "Hey Billie, that surgeon from the hospital's on the phone. Says he'd like to talk to you."

Rubie raised an eyebrow, "Oh yeah?"

Cursing her redheaded nature of blushing, Billie stumbled to her feet, and studiously ignored Rubie's laugh. When she got to the front desk, she paused for a moment, to give her time to collect herself, and then answered. "Hello?"

"Hi Billie, it's me, Mark."

"Hi Mark." She heard barely hidden muttering in the background and stifled a giggle. Kafia was clearly directing this phone call. "How can I help you?"

"*No, I'm not saying-* Ahem," he cleared his throat to try and distract from the tiny overlord speaking more than a little loudly next to him. Kafia had clearly had enough, because the next thing Billie heard was a scuffle and then the young girl's voice very loudly in her ear.

"Mark is going to take you to the cinema."

"*The cinema...why would I-*"

"Hush, Mark. Are you there, Billie?"

"I'm here."

"What would you like to see at the cinema?"

Billie pondered the question for a moment. She knew what she really wanted to see, but that was more than a little childish. However, a six-year-old was running the conversation. "What do *you* think we should go see?"

The named princess film brought a bark of laughter from the clearly put-upon Mark, and Billie agreed enthusiastically. "That sounds excellent. He may pick me up from work after six."

"Billie?" Mark had clearly managed to wrest control of the situation back from Kafia, and he sounded so dejected, that she almost laughed at his forlorn tone.

"I really would like to see that film."

"Then I would like to take you to see it." His voice warmed just as Rubie turned the corner, and Billie's face flared red once more.

The rest of the day flew by, and she threw herself into work. If she focused on what she was doing, she wouldn't have to worry about the fact that she'd forgotten to put makeup on that morning, or that she was wearing a dress that was more floaty than professional.

Rubie insisted on doing her makeup for her, and when Billie looked at herself in the mirror, she gasped. "What did you do?"

She was under no illusions as to how pretty she was. Sammie had been the one blessed with good looks. Billie'd been blessed with hair that didn't even curl, no matter how many times she tried co-washing it, and a face that could best be described as 'interesting'.

That wasn't to say that she didn't like the way she looked, but it did mean that she used her clothes to get people to remember her, and that people usually used contouring to draw out sharp angles in her face that weren't really there to begin with.

Rubie hadn't done that.

Instead, she'd done some kind of magic with a makeup brush that Billie now officially viewed as a wand, and made her look *soft*. It was shimmery, and drew attention to the roundness in Billie's face that she'd never quite loved before. But now it suited her, suited the soft pastels of her skirt, and the shimmeriness of her shoes, and made her realise that she looked pretty damn good.

"You'll text me, and let me know how it all goes?" pressed Rubie, and Billie had nodded.

The other woman had even insisted on opening the door and would have grilled Mark within an inch of his life, if Billie hadn't interjected and pulled him out towards the street.

She was quiet whilst they waited for the bus, as was he, until she snuck a look at him, from underneath her eyelashes, and he laughed at her.

"You okay there?"

She nodded, her words not ready just yet.

"Good," and he held out his hand for her to hold and this felt different. She didn't feel stressed, like she normally did; there was no wanting to pull back, to hide from his touch.

There'd been a reason why she'd hidden in the corner with books as Sammie held court, all those years ago. Just as her sister had basked under attention, it felt too much for Billie. She could feel people looking at her, their voices too loud, their touch too prickly, and everything about other people made her want to retreat into a cocoon of safety.

Mark didn't make her feel like that, which was a surprise, considering their first interaction.

She slipped her hand into his and squeezed experimentally. He squeezed back, and that traitorous flush stained her cheeks once more.

On the bus, he'd sat down first, and had given her the

option of sitting opposite him, but she sat beside him, and had found herself almost cuddling up to him.

"Do you mind if I put my arm here?" Mark had asked, leaning it along the back of her seat, and she'd grinned and told him that he could put it round her waist if he wanted.

So he had, and that had made her flush all over again.

"My goodness you're pretty when you're all shy."

That had her suspicious. "Pretty? I'm interesting looking, not really pretty," but even as she spoke the words, Billie knew that they weren't quite true. She'd seen her pretty softness in the mirror before she'd come out, and she looked adorable. But before she could correct her words, he took her chin in his fingers and turned her face to look at him.

"You're pretty, Billie. Very pretty."

Fine. Who was she to argue?

4

After the cinema, Mark offered to take her home.

She liked that, that he'd asked and not insisted. She knew that some people considered it gentlemanly, even a must, but she'd always felt that people who demanded to know where you lived seemed more than a little creepy.

But Mark had offered, and then suggested paying for a cab if she didn't feel comfortable.

She felt comfortable, and they clambered into a taxi together.

Billie had spent the entire film curled up next to him, as he'd picked a cinema that had sofas instead of the standard movie chairs, and he'd held her hand and even fed her popcorn. It had been swoonworthy levels of lovely.

He hadn't kissed her yet though.

"Mark?"

"Yes, Billie?"

"Why haven't you kissed me yet?"

Light from streetlamps flickered across his face as the car headed down the road, and she saw a half smile dance upon his lips.

"I wasn't sure that you wanted me to kiss you."

She nudged him with her shoulder playfully. "I want you to kiss me. Please."

"Aren't you a good girl, asking me so nicely?"

Billie squeezed her thighs together, and nodded her head vigorously.

Mark's chuckle then was low and throaty, and she felt it reverberate all the way down to her clit. He dropped his voice, so the driver couldn't hear, and leaned forward to whisper in her ear. "You like it when I call you good girl?"

"Yes." She breathed out the word, feeling almost giddy.

"Well, that makes sense, because you're clearly a very well-behaved little girl indeed."

Her gasp hitched in her throat, and he swore under his breath before leaning in and capturing her lips with his own. Billie melded her body to his, her arms moving unbidden to fall about his neck, and gave herself over to the kiss.

For a moment, everything stopped. There was nothing in the world but the two of them, hands clasping, stroking, caressing and when he pulled back, she followed him. Yearning for another kiss, the touch of his lips.

The cab pulled up outside her apartment block.

"You can come up, if you like," Billie said, and kissed him impetuously.

The walk up the flights of stairs felt like it lasted years, but then they were at her door, and she was unlocking it and *oh* his arms were back round her and he was walking her until her back was flat against the wall and he was kissing her again.

It wasn't until he kissed her neck though, his mouth and teeth teasing her skin, that she moaned "Daddy".

The word almost undid him and he buried his face in the nape of her neck and stilled for a moment, muttered words buffering her skin, until she tugged at him to meet her eyes.

"Do you mind? Me calling you Daddy, that is?"

His pupils had dilated, like they were desperate to take in every inch of her, and he gathered her face in his hands and kissed her more gently than she'd ever been kissed. "Oh darling, of course I don't mind you calling me Daddy. Have you had a Daddy before?"

Billie grinned at him, and turned the light on.

Her entire home was pastel, all pinks and lilacs and baby blues. Daddy Mark took it all in with a smile, and then scooped her up in his arms. "Which way to the princess's turret?"

She giggled and pointed him in the right direction, holding on tightly with her other hand. When he placed her on the bed, he did so carefully, before standing back and casting a glance around the room. "Ah ha!"

He reached over to her dresser, where a beautiful tiara made of pearls lay, and picked it up. "A princess has to wear a crown."

And then she was all waterfalling giggles and laughs, joy bubbling up and over, until she reached out for him. "Kiss me Daddy, please."

He kicked off his shoes, and slowly, carefully undid the laces of her little ankle boots.

"*Daddyyyyyyyyyyy…*" she whined.

Leaning forward, Daddy Mark nipped the inside of her thigh, just above the knee. "Good things come to princesses who wait."

"Fine." She pretended to sulk, but really Billie was delighted. She knew that she was shy, and that most of the time she wanted nothing more than to hide away, but her Little side was cheerful and more than a little bit sassy. "What good things?"

"Well…" Daddy Mark rolled down her socks, and then

ran a finger up the inside of her leg, pausing at the hem of her skirt.

She wriggled, and moved the skirt higher.

His finger followed, and then stopped at the hemline again.

"Daddy, that's not fair! I want kisses and and and *all the good things.*"

He moved up the bed, until he was on his side beside her, his fingers tracing lazy patterns on her upper thigh. "What do you think the good things could be, baby girl?"

Billie screwed up her face in thought. "I don't know. Whatever you think they should be!"

Daddy Mark chuckled, "You want me to decide?"

When she got like this, she didn't want to have to think, didn't want to have to make decisions. All she wanted was to let her head empty of all the big anxious thoughts, and let someone else decide for her. "Please."

"In that case I think they could be…kisses?"

She nodded, and he kissed her, peppering her face with kisses before capturing her lips. Billie melted beneath him and sighed happily.

"And they might also be…tickles?"

That made her shake her head vigorously, but he tickled her anyway, and then held her in her arms as she tried to catch her breath again from all the laughing.

"And also," here his fingers resumed their dance, just below the hem of her skirt, "do you think they might be fingers making you feel nice?"

"Oh," she breathed, and suddenly nothing was more important to her than having him touch her clit, having his fingers dip inside her wet hotness and fill her up. "Please Daddy."

"Please what?"

But she was too shy to use her words, so instead she

reached down to his wrist, and moved his hand up up until his fingers grazed the gusset of her underwear.

"Wow, princess, you're very drippy."

She'd been drippy since that first kiss, but she didn't quite know how to say that. Instead, she nuzzled her face against him shyly, as his fingers ran up and down, teasing her clit beneath the material.

"Oh no, princess, you're going to have to do better than that. Say it."

"I'm Daddy's drippy princess."

And then with one swift move he ripped the gusset of her knickers and slid his fingers into her hot, wet centre.

"I'll replace your knickers," he said.

"Daddy, I don't care." Because she didn't. The cool air sudden against her skin, and then the heat of his fingers, filling her up, was everything.

Daddy Mark kissed her again, nipping at her bottom lip and she moaned, writhed beneath him, beneath his fingers, feeling all the tension that had built up escalate until she was right on the edge.

"Please, Daddy."

"Please what, princess?"

"Please can I come?"

His eyes were warm as he gazed down at her. "Not yet princess."

Her cry was strangled and she grasped at the remnants of her control, determined not to go over the edge until he told her to.

"Daddy," she whispered.

"I got you princess," his fingers slowed inside her, no longer sliding in and out, but instead moving slowly, carefully, deeper, until he did something – she knew not what – a tiny movement of sorts and she was gasping and clutching at him and then, "Now, princess."

And she let go.

His fingers sent her hurtling over the edge, and his lips caught her cries and then her tears as she came again and again, the movement inside of her too much for her to bear.

When she came down from whatever dizzy heights she'd been inhabiting, he picked her up, and moved so that she could sit, curled up in his lap, whilst he rocked her back and forth.

"Thank you, Daddy."

"You're welcome baby."

5

Billie had been so euphoric the following day, when she'd walked into the office, her favourite multicoloured llama peeking out of her handbag, where Daddy Mark had popped it that morning, that Rubie had announced that she too would come to the unveiling of the new teddies at the children's hospital.

"I want to properly meet the man who's put such a smile on our Billie's face."

Our Billie. She hadn't been 'our Billie' since Sammie died. She swallowed, and then let her fingers graze against her llama.

Sammie had picked out the llama for her, a birthday present that she'd managed to corral a nurse into picking up for her. Billie had been assured that there'd been a budget and a plan, and of course there had been. Sammie was great at planning adventures.

Sammie would have liked Daddy Mark; would have teased him about his good looks, and her about the way that she blushed when she saw him. And would most definitely have approved of the fact that he seemed to like looking after

Billie. "Everyone looks after me," she'd said one night, when they were alone, watching tv and eating ice cream together. "Someone needs to look after you."

No-one really looked after Billie. They tried, but Sammie had taken precedent and then after… After no-one had been much good at anything. And her previous boyfriends and girlfriends had been great at sex and calling her cute, but they'd never really made her feel held.

No-one had rocked her to sleep until Daddy Mark.

And now here was Rubie, declaring Billie one of them, and Tillie and Jamie nodding along seriously.

It was nice, feeling part of something.

So, when they all turned up at Llama Ward the following day, greeted by excited children and tired parents, she'd felt a bit better when Rubie had slipped her hand into Billie's and squeezed. "It's okay to feel a little sad too," the other woman whispered. "You don't have to be smiley all the time."

They'd handed out the bears to each of the children on the ward, and Billie had offered to take additional pictures, for the families only, of each child with their bear. One bear had a neon green mohawk, and Jamie had attached a mini prosthetic leg to another. And Kafia's had been carefully shaven, and a scar sewn across its chest.

"That's like my open-heart surgery," she explained earnestly to Billie. "And look! It matches mine perfectly!" She threw off her top, which landed on her bemused mother's head, and proudly showed how the stitching and the scarring mirrored each other.

"They did an excellent job," said Billie. And then, because it had been so popular the last time, magicked cake out of thin air until all the children were distracted by bears and cake, and she could step back for a moment and take a breath.

"Hey princess." Daddy Mark's voice was very quiet, discrete, so no-one could hear.

"Hey." She smiled up at him, not saying 'Daddy' out loud, but both of them hearing it.

"You guys have done a great job. The kids love the bears."

She nodded, and then felt for her llama. It had been there for her, for so many years, but now Billie felt like he belonged here.

"Matron?" she asked, turning to the older woman. "I don't suppose the ward has a mascot? Sammie-" Her voice cut off, but Daddy Mark smiled at her, and Rubie nodded at her across the room, and she knew that she didn't need her llama to feel loved anymore. And besides, Sammie would always be with her. "I have a llama for the llama ward."

Matron Okoro took the stuffie from her, and hugged her. "Sammie would love this."

"She would." Then, as the older woman went to place the llama on the nurses' station, where everyone could see him, Billie reached out her hand and Daddy Mark took it. "And I love you, I think."

He leaned forward and kissed her gently, to the delight of the children. "I love you too, princess."

A
London Little's
MOO

ELLIE ROSE

❧ 6 ❧

Tillie looked anxiously round the pub. No sign of them yet.

She shuffled from foot to foot and allowed herself a discreet anxious stim. Fluttering fingers. No one noticed fluttering fingers when they were by her side. Well. No one apart from Alex.

The woman behind the bar smiled at her, and Tillie gave back an approximation of a smile. "You okay?"

"Yes, I'll have an orange juice, please."

The woman nodded, and as she got some ice for Tillie's glass, added, "I know the people who run the munch; I can ask someone to come down and meet you here, if you're nervous."

Tillie flushed, and her fluttering fingers stilled for a moment.

"It's okay," the woman smiled. "I've been around enough Littles to recognise the signs, and it is the monthly Littles munch. I'm Anna." She handed over Tillie's drink and stretched out her hand for Tillie to shake.

"Tillie," mumbled Tillie, and she did a quick shake. "And

thank you, but my Alex will be here in a moment." She looked towards the door again, "Hopefully."

Anna nodded, and then gestured towards one of the bar stools. "Why don't you hope up there whilst I take your payment, and you wait for your Caregiver? We can chat and I can make sure that no one bothers you that you don't want to bother you."

Handing over her card, Tillie clambered onto the stool, and wriggled around until she found the perfect fit for her bum. "Thank you."

The older woman was warm and friendly, and that was nice, but Tillie didn't really know what to do with warm and friendly people who weren't Alex. There was a reason that out of the two in-house designers at Stuffie Hospital London, Essie was the one who usually worked with children and the more loud and outgoing clients that they had. Tillie had managed to specialise in being the quiet and withdrawn one, which made her perfect for working with their more exclusive and private clients.

Most extroverts made Tillie want to hide away, and let them have centre stage, but not Alex. Alex was very loud, and high energy, but they felt like Tillie's very own personal ray of sunshine, and she'd have basked in their light all day and all night if she could.

Alex was also more than a little chaotic, so Tillie wasn't really surprised that they were running late, though they'd usually drop her a text, to let her know.

Just then, the door of the pub swung open, and Alex ran into the pub and up to where Tillie was seated, completely out of breath. They bent over and panted, and Tillie rolled her eyes and asked Anna for a glass of tap water with ice.

They grinned gratefully and gulped it down before turning to her and grasping her hands in theirs. "Tills, I'm so so sorry. I forgot to charge my phone in the office, cos ADHD, and I missed my bus and then it died as I was texting to tell you." A deep in-breath. They weren't done. "You know that I'd never have forgotten you, right? And I'm here, of course I'm here." A dashing smile blinded Anna, who looked vaguely stunned. "And you look, holy crap Tills, you look adorable!"

Tillie looked down at her pastel rainbow pinafore dress and gave an awkward smile. "Yeah yeah."

"*Yeah yeah,*" parroted Alex, "More like *hell yeah!*" They tugged at her to get off the chair, held her hand and got her to spin on the spot. "There we go, my little grump, perfect."

She flushed. It wasn't that she didn't like my little grump; she actually liked it a lot. Too much, in fact. Alex was only her faux Caregiver for the evening, so she didn't have to come to the munch alone. Unfortunately, her traitorous heart hadn't got the message.

Tillie couldn't help herself. She looked up at the taller enby and stuck her tongue out.

That was surprising.

She wasn't usually the kind of Little who bratted. She didn't like bratting. She liked being a good girl. The kind of girl who got showered with praise, so she never had to worry about getting told off. And the last thing she'd ever want to do would be to piss Alex off.

But somehow, for some reason, this kind of felt right.

Alex raised their eyebrows, picked up Tillie's empty glass, and sniffed. "What've you been drinking then, Tilliebean? Naughty juice?"

Out of the corner of her eye, Tillie could see Anna fighting back a laugh. "Nope, just orange juice." She frowned. Damn it, that wasn't back-chatty enough. "Silly Zeze." There you go. That would do it.

A look flitted across Alex's face that she'd never seen

before and Tillie wondered for a split second if she'd pushed them too far.

Instead, Alex turned to look at Anna. "No more naughty juice for Miss Tilliebean here, just water, I think," and then they turned back to Tillie and offered them a challenging look.

"But…but…but…" Tillie humphed and even stamped her foot. "That's not *fair*."

"Neither is calling your Zeze silly, is it?"

She screwed up her face into a scowl and muttered under her breath.

Alex laughed and ruffled her hair.

This was…this was…

Different.

That's what it was, different. And fun different as well.

Tillie scowled some more, but only to keep a grin from spreading across her face. She could be naughty, and Alex didn't seem to mind. Not too much, at least.

Not for the first time, she wondered what it would be like to have Alex as her Zeze for real. They were funny, kind, didn't mind her moods and grumps, and gave the best cuddles in the world. Tillie would go to the stars and back for her sunshiny friend, but that didn't mean that they saw her in the same way. At least, not romantically.

That thought brought her back down to earth with a bump, and she felt her bottom lip begin to tremble a bit.

She always tried not to think about Alex too hard when she was Little, because of just this reason. Sometimes it made her sad and she wanted to cry. The last thing she wanted to do was have a meltdown in the pub.

But Alex noticed her trembly lip, reached into their bag, and brought out a Tupperware container full of diced fruit. They glanced apologetically at Anna, "I hope that's okay, but if she doesn't eat…"

"I've had Littles of my own," Anna waved her hand. "Fruit away."

They popped the lid, and handed Tillie a fork with cute farmyard animals on it. She paused to look at them, and then down at the fork. It was covered in cows; her very favourite of all farmyard animals. Heartache momentarily forgotten, she beamed at Alex. "Look Zeze, it has moos on it!"

"So it does Tilliebean, now have your fruit. No wobbly lips for my little grump."

She wriggled back onto the barstool and hoovered her way through the container. Yummy. And actually, exactly what she needed. She'd had lunch, but had only nibbled at her food as she'd been so nervous about this evening, and about the munch.

The munch!

Alex clocked the moment when she realised, and went to get down from the stool, but their hand held her sternly in place. "Where do you think you're going, little one?"

"We're late for the munch! It's upstairs!"

They tutted, and gently nudged the fork in Tillie's hand back towards the last few blueberries. "Fruit first, and then we'll go upstairs. Okay?"

Tillie settled back down, and Anna looked between them, smiled and went to deal customers at the other end of the bar.

"Hey Tills," Alex's voice sounded nervous and she looked up at them, all wide-eyed blinking innocence.

"Yes?"

"Is this okay? I'm doing it right?" They ran a hand through their short hair, unintentionally showing off their undercut and Tillie almost melted at the sight.

"You're doing great! A lot better than some of my previous Caregivers have done."

That made Alex pull a face. "Yes, well, we've spoken about

you dating twits. Not allowed. Being nice to you should be your baseline in a relationship, Tilliebean, not something you settle for living without."

"It's not as simple as that-" she began, but they leaned forward until their forehead was almost touching hers.

"I swear you'll be the death of me. Yes, Tillie, it is just as simple as that. Damn it, maybe I should take you out on some proper dates, show exactly how it is that you should be treated, so you don't settle for anything less."

Tillie blinked furiously. "What?"

"Yes," Alex said, more decisively, standing straight again. "I think that would be a good idea. What do you think?"

"Yes?"

"'Yes?' or 'Yes!'?"

"Yes." Her voice sounded determined, even as her pulse raced and her heart beat a veritable tarantella in her chest.

"And I'm already your Zeze for the night, so let's start now. Come on babygirl, let's go upstairs."

$ 7 $

For all that she'd been excited for the munch, Tillie was in a slight state of shock.

The last thing she'd expected was for Alex to suggest that they date, and they were clearly quite serious about it. The two of them had pre-agreed safewords when Alex had agreed to be Tillie's Zeze for the night, so she could stop at any time, but she wanted it to never end.

That was dangerous thinking; she knew that. But Alex had held her hand all the way up the stairs, and when they'd entered the function room, they'd taken her over to the play corner, because they could sense she was nervous.

There were other Littles there, including Jamie, from work. Tillie's eyes had gotten big, and she'd taken a few steps backwards until she'd come up against the hard lines of Alex's body behind her.

"You okay there, Tilliebean?" Alex whispered in her ear.

She shook her head.

"What's the matter? Come on, use your words for me, sweetheart."

"Is scary," she mumbled.

"Well, why don't I come and play with you then." And before she knew what was happening, Alex was sat on the carpet next to Jamie, and was picking up some farmyard animals to play with.

Shyly, she edged over and knelt behind the two of them, determined not to draw attention to herself. It was nice, seeing all of the toys, but she felt a bit overwhelmed. There were a lot of people, mainly people she didn't know, and lots of noise. It felt a bit like a wall picking itself up and slamming into her, over and over and over again.

She rocked a little bit on the spot, and couldn't help but whine a little.

Alex glanced at her over their shoulder, and their entire face softened. "Come here, little one, come and play with me and Jamie."

Jamie's face lit up when he saw her. "Tillie! I didn't know you were coming to this tonight."

She mumbled something in reply, and to her horror, her thumb made its way to her mouth. She frowned at it, and would have shoved it away, if Alex hadn't brushed her hair from her face, and pulled her into their lap. She wriggled and then started sucking her thumb, the action soothing.

"Tilliebean is a little bit nervous, Jamie," they explained. "It's her first time at a munch like this."

Jamie nodded sagely. "It can be quite scary when you're on your own, but it's nice that you have Alex here, to help you."

Tillie took her thumb from her mouth long enough to say "They're my Zeze," before putting it back in and sucking again.

Alex's arms were warm about her, and she felt cuddled and cherished and safe.

With her free hand, she reached out to grab a cow from Jamie's pile.

The sharp tap on her knuckles made her blink tears away, and look at Alex in horror.

"You have to say please, baby girl."

She almost grumped, but didn't when she saw the look of admonishment on their face. "I'm sorry Jamie."

"That's okay Tillie, we can play together if you like?"

"Okay."

As they played at farms—Tillie got to look after all of the moos—she found herself unwinding more and more. She liked Jamie, though she hadn't really spoken much to him at work before, and this was actually nice, getting to be Little with someone else who was also a Little. But the best thing about the whole evening, was Alex's presence. Solid. Calm. Safe.

Previous Daddies she'd been with hadn't really been interested in playing. They just wanted her to be a good girl and do as she was told, and though she *could* do that, Tillie had a sneaking suspicion that that wasn't really what she wanted at all.

As the evening wore on, the noise started grating at her more and more, and her hands shook as she tried to find her earplugs in her bag. They wouldn't shut out everything, she'd still be able to talk to Jamie and Zeze—wow, she was already thinking of Alex as Zeze— but they would dampen the sound in the rest of the room.

When she found them, she breathed a sigh of relief, before putting them in and screwing her eyes shut.

"Hey Tilliebean," Alex's voice was quieter now, filtered as it was through the earplugs, "You doing okay?"

"Can I have a cuddle?" she whispered, and when they nodded yes, she wrapped her arms around them and buried her face against them.

Taking a breath, Tillie tried to regulate her breathing. In for four, hold for four, out for four, hold for four. It was one of her reset exercises. She'd developed a couple of them with her therapist. Another good one was running her wrists under cold water but there wasn't a sink in sight.

She knew that she should let go of Alex and sit up, that she shouldn't let her own issues bleed out into the evening and affect them, but when she loosened her arms, they just held her tighter, and she fell back against them quietly.

"Come on babygirl," Alex said. "Say goodbye to Jamie; I think it's time for you to go home."

Tillie wanted to stomp her feet and say no, refuse to leave, but she was just so *tired*, and so she whispered a goodbye in Jamie's direction.

He leaned over and hugged her impulsively. "I'll see you at work tomorrow?"

She nodded.

"And Tillie?"

"Yes."

"Make sure you have some aftercare this evening. Just being in Littlespace around other people can trigger subdrop, if you're not used to it."

She flushed, but nodded shyly. "Twas nice seein' you."

"And you!"

And then Alex was gathering her and her things up, uncurling her fingers from where she had them clenched around a toy moo, and bustling her out of the room and down the stairs.

Anna was still at the bar as they came down into the main room of the pub. "Have a good time?"

Alex answered for them both, and Tillie found that she really didn't mind. "Nice, but I think this one's tired herself out. Time for bed, I think."

"Ni'night, Anna," Tillie said sleepily.

"Night night, Tillie," she replied.

Alex must have bundled them both into an uber, because

before she knew it, Tillie was at her front door, and Alex was getting her keys out of her bag.

They'd been round her flat hundreds, maybe thousands, of times before, but they still paused at the step until she invited them in.

Her flat, the ground floor apartment in an old converted row of terraced houses, was surprisingly big for a London flat. It helped that she was right at the end of the Jubilee line, as far out from Central London as you could get before merging into Hertfordshire. A small kitchen, smaller bedroom, and decent sized living room. And her bathroom which had an actual bath in it. Tillie thought that she'd expire if she ever had to give up bubble baths.

Alex steered her towards the bedroom and she stopped and looked at them. "What're you doing?"

"Getting you ready for bed, babygirl. And then maybe, once you've brushed your teeth and gotten all tucked in, I might read you a story."

"Can it be *Peter Rabbit?*"

When they smiled at her, she thought her heart might burst, she was so happy. "Of course."

She practically skipped into her bedroom then, getting changed into cute little cow print pyjamas, and then running to brush her teeth.

"Are you going to get into bed with me Zeze?"

Alex looked conflicted. "I think perhaps I sit on top of the covers to read to you, and then sleep on the sofa, babygirl."

Tillie was confused. "But you always crash in my bed when you stay over."

"Yes, but I've never been Zeze before."

Her pulse beat that little bit faster, and she nodded slowly. It was okay, she tried telling herself, it didn't mean that Alex didn't like her. Just that they didn't like her like *that*. And their friendship was far too important to risk.

"Okay." Her voice was very quiet, quieter than usual, Alex looked like they wanted to curse.

"Okay, how about we make a deal? I'll stay in the bed as usual, but just cuddles. A good Zeze doesn't rush their Little into anything, especially when they're so deep in Littlespace that they can't quite think straight."

Tillie's pulse evened out and the sigh she let out relaxed her entire body. "I can do that!" Bouncing up onto the bed, she crawled down and got under the covers. "Story now!"

"Who knew you were so bratty?" said Alex with a short laugh.

"You love me being bratty, so if I'm being bratty, that *actually* makes me a good girl," retorted Tillie.

"Gotta love a brat's logic, now, what do you say Tilliebean?"

"Story now!" she paused dramatically, "*Pleeeeeeeease.*"

But she didn't even make it to the end of Peter Rabbit's adventures before she was fast asleep, curled up in Alex's arms.

❧ 8 ❧

When the sun broke through Tillie's window, dancing beams upon her face, she was more than a little confused at how heavy her duvet felt. Until she looked at said duvet, and realised that the weight was little more than Alex's arm, anchoring her to them.

She wriggled a little, trying to break free, and then gave up, stubbornly stuck.

"Oi."

Nothing.

"Alex!"

Still nothing.

The naughtiest thought crept into her mind, and she wriggled close until she got slightly shift, her mouth to their ear.

"*Aaaaaaaaaaaaaaaaah!*"

Alex sat bolt upright, head moving from side to side urgently. "Wha-? What the-?" And then their gaze fell upon Tillie, who was laughing so hard she'd fallen onto her back and was rolling around. "You little minx!"

And then they fell upon her and tickled her until she

couldn't breathe, and only stopped when Tillie's bedside alarm went off.

After they'd taken turns showering, they sat on Tillie's sofa, munching on toast, and talking about the day ahead.

"So," said Alex, when a natural lull in the conversation occurred, "How did you find last night?"

"The munch?"

"Well, yes the munch, but also, our first date."

Tillie flushed. "The munch was good. Very loud though; I think I'd prefer small playdates with other Littles than going somewhere that loud again."

"And…?"

"And what?" She grinned at them cheekily.

Alex shook their head and looked at Tillie in such a way that made her behave pretty darn quickly.

"And it was nice. You're really good as a Zeze; I'm surprised you haven't done it before." It had been a lovely surprise to see how well they'd slipped into that role, teasing her, looking after her, cajoling her when necessary.

"I've never had anyone who needed looking after like that before."

That made Tillie feel slightly uncomfortable, and she wriggle in place, to try and get some of the discomfort to dissipate.

"You okay there?"

"Yeah, I'm fine."

It was clearly a lie, and the words sat between them until Tillie wished that she could reel them back in.

"Want to try that again?"

"No."

Alex raised their eyebrows at her. "Okay, well, we need to go to work, or we're going to be late. But if you think that I'm going to drop this, think again. No lying, Tills."

Something scrunched in her chest and Tillie thought she

might be sick. Forget butterflies, it was as if she had a swarm of birds racing round and round her insides. It was a horrible feeling, and no matter what she did throughout the rest of the day, they wouldn't go away. And she tried all sorts of things.

She tried starting a new project—stomach still swarmed.

She went out for a walk at lunch—stomach still swarmed.

She even had a meeting with Billie to work on the next project with the local children's ward—Stomach. Still. Swarmed.

Nothing she did changed it.

So Tillie was stuck with two shitty realisations: one, that she really couldn't lie to Alex without feeling terrible about it; and two, that she was going to have to tell Alex the truth about how she'd felt that morning.

Knowing how she felt wasn't a problem, but telling them about it…now that was something that she really didn't want to have to do.

Alex had said that she needed looking after. And in theory, that wasn't a problem. She knew that Littles needed looking after; that headspace made them vulnerable, and they needed to protect their Little side at all costs, but it wasn't the first time someone had said something like that about her. Only their tone had been completely different.

One of her exes had never wanted her to go out to bars or the pub with him, because he said that she needed looking after too much, that it meant that he couldn't enjoy himself or have a nice time if she was there. He couldn't relax because she needed looking after, and those words imprinted themselves on her brain.

Before she knew it, she equated being looked after with being a burden, and that was the last thing she'd want to be to anyone. She didn't want to be work, a chore, something someone merely put up with, and the idea of putting the burden of her onto Alex…

Tillie shuddered. She could think of nothing worse.

This was a bad idea. Them fake dating was a bad idea, because if Alex truly realised who she was, what hard work she was, they'd never want to be her friend again, and she couldn't lose them. They were far too important to her.

She worked herself up into such a state that when Jamie popped into her office that afternoon, she'd looked at him with red-rimmed eyes, and the other man had immediately closed the door and sat down on a chair beside Tillie.

"Tillie, what's the matter?"

But by this point words were quite beyond her, and she merely shook her head as tears rolled down her cheeks.

"I'm getting Alex-"

"*No!*"

Jamie lowered himself back into the seat slowly. "Fuck, Tillie, what happened? If they-"

"No, nothing like that, I just-" her breath was staccato now, jaggedly punctuating her words. "I can't let them see me like this. It's too much. *I'm* too much."

Jamie slid himself out of the chair, and tugged at her hands until Tillie sat down on the floor next to him. "I don't think you're too much."

She looked at him, wide-eyed. "Really? I'm sat on the floor in my office, crying in the middle of the day. That's the very definition of being too much, isn't it?"

He shook his head. "That's not too much. I'm still here, aren't I?"

He was right. He was still here. She choked back a sob. "Yes, because you're a nice person. You shouldn't have to put up with this."

Jamie shuffled closer, and put an arm around her. "I cry on my own sometimes, and it's really sad. I don't mind holding you if you need to cry; I'd rather that, than you cry on your own."

She wiped her eyes with the back of her fingers, and looked at him. "Why do you cry?"

"Because I'm lonely and because someone hurt me. Why are you crying?"

Instead of blurting out that it was because she was too much again, Tillie stopped and thought about it. *Really* thought about it.

"I think," she said, faltering as the words formed slowly in her mind. "I think I'm crying because someone hurt me too. And because I'm scared of being lonely."

Jamie nodded. "But don't you have Alex? The two of you are always together, and they came with you to the munch last night."

"I do have Alex, but I'm scared that if they see me like this too much—all big emotions, big reactions, big mess—then they'll decide that they don't want me in their life anymore."

Her colleague looked thoughtful. "That doesn't seem like the kind of person Alex is, or the kind of thing that they'd do."

"I think I know that, deep down, but for some reason my body really doesn't, and so I have these horrible get-ready-for-disaster butterflies in my stomach that *just won't leave.*" She found herself tightening her hands into little angry fists, and she realised that she wanted to hit something, anything. Fuck. She wanted to throw a tantrum, here, in the middle of her office.

The realisation siphoned off some of the angry energy and she slumped, leaning against Jamie. "It's really not fair," she whispered. "It's not fair that it's so hard."

"I know," he said, and squeezed her. "It does get easier though." There was a sadness, deep in his blue eyes that made her heart ache in recognition. He really did understand, and maybe it did get easier. "I find that therapy helps," he added.

"I do therapy," she said, "but apparently it doesn't stop the feels, which is *wrong*." Tillie was turning all that ache and pain into humour now. Easier to break the tension. "I really think that after a certain number of months, your body should get a note that it no longer freaks out."

There was a knock on her office door, and then Alex popped their head round. They took in the sight of the two Littles on the floor, cuddling, and Tillie's tear-stained face, and entered sharpish. "Tills, what's the matter?"

Jamie disentangled himself gently, and got up. "I think I'm going to let you two talk," he said. "Tillie, you've got my extension number if you need it?"

She nodded, and hiccupped. "Thank you, Jamie."

"Any time."

As he closed the door behind them, Alex went to sit on the floor next to her but she shook her head. "On the chair please." And then scooted over so that she could sit at their feet, rest her head on their knees, and not have to look them in the eyes at all.

This was going to be hard.

"I don't want to be a burden," she blurted out, never looking at Alex's face. There was an imperceptible shift in their body, and she was torn between checking to see what they were thinking, and not wanting to know what they thought. "I know that I'm a lot, and that I'm high maintenance, but I can't help it sometimes. And I don't want that to overshadow our friendship. So I don't think we should fake date."

Alex was quiet for a long moment and Tillie almost forgot how to breath. "I'm not sure we should fake date either," they said. "I was actually going to talk to you tonight about proper dating."

The first statement stole Tillie's breath so suddenly that she thought she was going to throw up, and the second returned it so suddenly that she had a mini coughing fit.

Alex passed her the water bottle that sat on her desk, and waited patiently until she'd stopped coughing. "You're my best friend Tillie, and yes, you react differently to things than I do, but that's not a bad thing. What brought all of this on?"

"You said that you'd never had someone who needed looking after before."

"That doesn't mean I don't think that you're capable of looking after yourself." They gestured around the room. "Look at where you are, in your dream job. You're very capable indeed, but you also deserve to have someone who'll look after you sometimes. Everyone does. And-" Alex continued, before she could interrupt, "having needs is not a bad thing. Having needs and being able to express what those are is actually a real strength. It makes my life a little bit easier, knowing what it is that you want or need in a moment. And in those moments where you don't know, or your head or the world is too loud for you to work it out, I can help."

Tillie took a long gulp of water whilst she processed their words. "I know you believe it, but I might have moments of anxiety and moments when I worry about it a lot."

Alex stroked her hair and she leant back against their legs. "That's totally okay. And completely understandable considering some of the…specimens of humanity that you've dated in the past."

She giggled. The tightness in her chest was easing somewhat, and she could breathe without wanting to throw up.

"And how would you feel about actually dating me?"

Tillie didn't need to think about it. She'd been in love with Alex for so long that she knew her answer, but to actually date… "It's risky. If something went wrong, we could ruin our friendship."

"Some things are worth a little risk."

"Do you even fancy me?"

Alex's laugh was low and it reverberated through Tillie. "Do I-yes, Tilliebean. I fancy you."

"Huh." That was a surprise. "I didn't know."

"How about, after work, we go back to mine? We can order in takeaway, watch a film, and see if you fancy me too."

Tillie dipped her head to hide the flush across her cheeks. "I suppose I could be on board with that." She was *totally* on board with that.

❈ 9 ❈

Tillie knew Alex's flat almost as well as she knew her own. It was a lot smaller, being closer to the centre of town, and sat above a Bangladeshi restaurant, that always seemed to be wildly popular. Alex had popped downstairs, when the both of them had gotten in, and had returned with bags of the most delicious smelling food. and they'd settled down on the sofa to argue over what to watch and stuff their faces.

They'd settled on *My Big Fat Greek Wedding*, and had laughed their way through Toula's familial exploits and drama.

"It's got heart," declared Tillie, as the end credits rolled, waving a nimki around, "and her family might be slightly mad, but they love her."

"You've got to admit that it's fairly horrendous though," argued Alex, not willing to back down. "That they only want her to marry a Greek, and the way that her father talks about women…"

Tillie couldn't argue with that exactly, so she grinned and bit into the nimki. Yum. "So, what do we do now then?"

Alex looked at the remnants of the feast and waggled their eyebrows at her. "Well, we've done the takeaway and the film part…you finding me alluringly attractive yet?"

She saw through their bravado to the nervousness that lay beneath. "Yes," she said simply. "I always have." And that was it, the words were out there, with no way to take them back.

Tillie closed her eyes, focusing on keeping herself centred, and felt something brush against her lips. Her eyes flew open and Alex was there, face so close she could count each eyelash, if she so desired.

"Oh shit," said Alex, looking vaguely panicked. "I thought you were closing your eyes cos you wanted to be kissed."

There was an awkward silence, before they both burst out laughing.

"Why don't you try that again," suggested Tillie. "Now that I'm ready."

Alex cupped one side of her face with their hand, tilted their head and leaned in. This time their lips weren't so cautious; gentle pressure that caressed her skin and then—heavens—their other hand mirrored the first until her face was being held more tenderly than it had ever been held before.

Then those hands were sliding back until they tangled in Tillie's hair, tugging once, twice, and a third time unsuccessfully at the hairband that kept her unruly curls off her face. Their lips left hers, and they cursed under their breath as they battled with the elastic.

"Do you want some help?" asked Tillie, cheekily.

The look they shot her had her squirming where she sat. "No, I got this."

"Are you sure? Because it doesn't seem as if you got it."

Just as she spoke, the elastic came free, and with a squawk of triumph, Alex fisted Tillie's hair and pulled.

Fuck.

Tillie didn't even realise that she'd spoken out loud until Alex's irises grew large and dark, as if determined to take in every inch of her reaction. They pulled again, and she found herself moving to follow where they led, until she was astride their waist, skirt hitched up around her knees.

They thrust upwards and the ridge of their jeans rubbed against Tillie's underwear in just the right way and fuck she was going to come apart.

They pulled her hair once more, baring Tillie's neck and then kissed the sensitive skin.

"What's your safeword?"

"Huh?" Tillie was floating, barely aware of anything other than Alex's hands and mouth and why the fuck wasn't Alex's mouth on her anymore.

"Tills, what's your safeword?"

"Oh, traffic lights. Red, yellow green. And I'll tap out if my mouth is…" and here she let her gaze fix upon Alex's, "otherwise occupied."

They cursed and she giggle impetuously, delighted with the effect she had on them.

"I'll do the same, okay?"

"Sure. Now are you going to stop talking and actually *do* something?"

They moved their mouth from where it had been headed, and leaned back. "Someone's a little bratty this evening."

"Well yes, because there's all this talking happening, and not much kissing."

"What do you say?"

"Now."

They did *something*, Tillie knew not what, and then she was on her back beneath them. They loomed above her and she knew that she was wetter than she'd been in years. And they hadn't even done anything more than kiss her yet.

"And now?"

"Mark me." The words were a ghost of the depth of her desire, but Alex felt them the way that she did, Tillie could tell. "Mark me and make me yours."

"You are mine."

She felt Alex's response all the way down to her toes, and then they bent their head, nudging at her until she let hers fall to the side, and they licked at her neck.

"Here?"

"Yes."

"What's the magic word?"

Tillie considered bratting for a moment, but she was too far gone to draw this out any further. "Please, Zeze, please mark me."

And then their mouth was hot against her skin, kissing and sucking and biting until she almost arched off the sofa from the pleasure. There was pain there too, a sharp sensation that grounded her in the here and now and kept her from floating away too easily. When Alex lifted their head and looked at the nape of her neck, they let out a low whistle.

"You're going to have a mark alright, Tilliebean."

She knew, she could feel it tingling. "Well, you can do *some* things right, at least."

They grabbed her legs flipped them up over their right shoulder in one swift move, and delivered a devastatingly stern spank to her bum.

"Ow!"

"That's what little grumps get, when they mouth off to their Zeze."

"Oh yeah? What else do they get?"

Alex's eyes sparkled. "You're about to find out."

$\maltese$ 10 $\maltese$

They hadn't quite carried Tillie to their bed, but there'd been a fair amount of being encouraged along by Alex's hand in her hair, and when she got to the edge of their bed, they pushed her forward until she fell atop the covers.

"All fours, please," they said.

"Four, forty-four, four hundred and forty-four…" began Tillie, feeling more than a little smug. She felt less smug, when a parry of spanks fell upon her arse.

"Get on all fours. Now."

She hurried into position, and then threw an attempted carefree glance over her shoulder at Alex. "That all you got?"

There was a pause this time, and then a blindfold was thrust into her hands.

"But I don't want-"

"You have your safeword babygirl. If you want me to stop, all you have to do is use it. Use yellow if you want to stop and talk about it."

There was a pause.

They both knew that she wasn't going to safeword, not over something as simple as a blindfold.

She put it on without another word.

There was a sound to the side of Alex pulling open a drawer, and a collection of somethings fell on the bed.

"I'm going to tell you what each of the things are, and I want you to red, yellow or green each implement."

"So I get to choose my punishment?"

Alex's laugh was short. "Not a chance, little miss grump; but you always get to say what you don't want. So red for absolutely not; yellow for not without prior agreement; and green for yes please, Zeze."

Air rushed past her face and there was a thump on the bed.

"Paddle. Leather."

"Yellow." She liked paddles, but needed a hell of a lot more build up to be able to thoroughly enjoy them.

"Flogger. Leather."

"Green, but have you got suede?" A myriad of different sounds hit her airs, and she felt a number of different implements hit the mattress beside her.

"I have many floggers; but I'll note your preference for suede."

A whistle by her ear had her shouting red almost immediately.

"No canes, Tilliebean?"

"Please no, Zeze."

They pressed a kiss to her forehead then, the imprint of their lips lingering long after the lips themselves. "Good girl."

"Pinwheels?"

That made her trembly, but she nodded, saying shakily, "Green, please."

"Please? Oh wow, that sounds like something you want. Is it?"

She felt shaky, as if her body were vibrating with anticipation. "Not exactly, Zeze."

"Use your words pretty girl."

"I like the sensation, as long as it's not pressed in."

The tiny pinpricks of metal rolled across the skin of her arm, as light as air, but still insistently there. Tillie moaned and started to physically tremble. Gentle fingers followed the pinwheel along its route, sharp and soft alternating until her entire skin felt like it was vibrating.

Alex sat on the bed next to her, and swept Tillie's hair from her face. "Hey there."

"Hi." Her voice sounded impossibly tiny.

"You're doing so well, Tilliebean."

"Thank you Zeze." Her words were floating on her breath now, dissipating into nothingness as soon as they left her lips.

"But there is a small matter of punishment to consider."

"Punishment?" she went to move, but a firm hand kept her in place.

"You lied to me this morning Tillie. It's okay to not know how you're feeling, or even to say that you need some time to think it through before talking about it, or even that you don't want to talk about it at all, but lying is not okay."

Behind the blindfold, Tillie felt tears gather on her lashes.

"Now, it's the first time you've ever lied to me, and I understand that it was a really big and scary topic for you, so I'm not angry. But in order for you to let this go-"

"Yes please." The words burst from Tillie's mouth. "I've been feeling horrible about it all day. Please can we do whatever it is you intend to do, so that I can let it go? Please Zeze?"

Alex kissed her forehead again and stood up, flipping up the back of Tillie's skirt. "You going to be a good girl and take your flogging?"

"Yes Zeze." Tillie reached out blindly for, something,

anything to hold onto, and found her fingers falling upon a soft toy.

Alex chuckled. "Trust you; I was going to give them to you as a reward for taking your punishment, but you can have them now, if you need something to hold onto."

"Yes please, Zeze."

"I'll introduce you properly after. You ready?"

"Yes Zeze."

They must have picked a suede flogger, because when the tails fell upon Tillie's skin, they felt soft. Beautifully, bitingly soft. She hissed through her teeth, and clung onto the stuffie in her hands.

"Good girl. I'm not going to get you to count, because I want you to concentrate on how it feels."

Thwack.

Damn, but Alex was good with that flogger. Not too hard, but certainly harder than the first.

"With each strike, I want you to let some of the fear that made you lie go. It's going to get further and further away from you each time I flog-" and the flogger came down *hard*, "-you."

And then the blows rained down on her arse in no discernible pattern or rhythm. Just over and over until she didn't quite know where she ended and the flogger begun.

When Alex started slowing down, making each strike more deliberate, increasingly intentional, Tillie finally began to sob. She let it all go, every semblance of control stripped from her until she was putty in her Zeze's hands.

They stopped then, dropping the flogger onto the floor beside the bed with a thump, and clambering atop the bed, to hold Tillie in their arms. They enveloped her body, and rocked her onto her side, so that they could spoon her, whispering over and over in her ear. "It's okay Tilliebean, you did so good. I'm so so proud of you. I've got you. It's okay."

At some point, they tugged the blindfold from Tillie's eyes, and she allowed herself to just curl up in Alex's arms, and let them gently rock her back and forth, tears flowing.

This time she didn't feel too much, or like she was being a burden. Alex had led her here, and encouraged her, and was holding her. It was okay, *she* was okay.

She glanced down at the stuffie, still clutched tightly in her hands, and gave a shaky smile.

Alex had gotten her a moo.

The next day was a Saturday. After the flogging, Alex had made Tillie drink far more water than was necessary, and have a snack, before getting her to brush her teeth and get into bed.

They'd kissed her again, gently and with so much love and care that Tillie had felt right at home. But then had insisted on sleep.

So it wasn't until Tillie woke up the next day, that she got more than just kisses.

She hadn't woken Alex up with a yell this time; hadn't need to. When she'd rolled over, they'd been lying there, watching her quietly. And the look in their eyes…it was all the impetus Tillie needed, to lean across and kiss the enby.

They discarded clothes quickly, tops pulled up and over, bottoms tugged off, socks kicked haphazardly off the bed until they lay facing each other, naked.

"I don't know," Tillie began, "I mean, I don't want to cause any gender dysphoria."

Alex smiled and kissed her slowly, their tongue darting

forth cautiously, as if they wanted to taste her. "Avoid my nips, and we'll be fine."

"And your…wrinkly bits?"

That made Alex shout with laughter. "Wrinkly-oh Tilliebean, you'll be the death of me. Pussy is fine. I have one and it doesn't upset me to have it called that. I'm pretty good with a strap-on though, and would probably prefer to fuck you, rather than you fucking me."

It was Tillie's turn to giggle. "I think that even if I were fingering you, if that's sumat you'd like, it would still feel like you were fucking me."

"That's because I would be." Their face lost its usual animated playfulness for a moment, softening as Alex ran a hand across Tillie's tits and down to where desire pooled between her thighs. "Oh Tills, you're slick."

"Well yes," Tillie said, slightly confused at the wonder in Alex's voice. "You're touching me like this, kissing me, of course I'm wet for you."

They coated their fingers in her wetness, and then traced circles around Tillie's clit that made her head spin. "Yeah you are." They kissed her then, stealing each moan and gasp she made for their own, and she was lost. Lost in the sensations that threatened to undo her completely. Lost to Alex.

"Please," she began murmuring, pleading quietly.

"Please what?"

"Please go inside me."

A low chuckle, and then one—no two—fingers slid inside her, stroking and moving until she could feel the base of Alex's hand against the entrance to her pussy.

"Oh *fuck* Zeze," and then she was keening, over and over "Zeze Zeze Zeze please please please," until Alex kissed her hard and said "Now," with a fierceness that she didn't recognise. But it didn't matter because she was coming apart, screaming the pleasure that Alex wrought from her until she went limp, and Alex withdrew their fingers.

Tillie lay still for a long time after that, for so long that Alex looked a little worried at one point and all she could do was wave and smile weakly, and cling on every time Alex went to move away. Finally, she was able to whisper, "Thank you Zeze."

"Thank me? Thank *you* babygirl. You are beautiful when you come."

She blushed and then slowly sat up. "Ummmm…may I…?"

"May you what?"

"May I please play with your pussy, Zeze?"

They smiled and lay back down next to her. "Of course you may, Tilliebean."

She reached out to where her glasses sat on the bedside table, perched them on her nose, and then shuffled, so she could sit cross-legged between her Zeze's legs.

Alex started to laugh, but she looked up and gave them her shhhh, I'm concentrating look, and went back to looking at the delight laid out before her.

The enby was wet, she could actually see that, and they shivered when she dipped her finger into the cream and used it to roll around their clit. That felt amazing, seeing Alex react to her like that, but nothing in the world had ever felt as good as Alex's pussy when she slipped her finger inside. It was hot and warm and "holy fuck."

"What?" Alex almost pushed themselves up onto their elbows before she shook her head at them.

"No no, it's just, your pussy is *amazing*. How did I not know how amazing your pussy is?"

Their answering laughter was a peal of surprised delight, "I'm glad you like it."

"I do, very much." She lifted her head and smiled. "Please may I make you come, Zeze."

Alex cursed and nodded, biting their lip, and she stroked with one hand, and thrust with the other, until the two hands, working in tandem brought Alex right to the edge. She could feel the enby's pussy tightening around her fingers, and she wanted—no *needed*—to make them come.

Tillie looked right at Alex, and smiled shyly. "Please come for me, Zeze," and with a strangled shout, that's exactly what they did, sitting up and leaning their forehead against hers as pleasure wracked their body.

Then they pulled her close and kissed her, lying them both down until they were comfortable together.

"See, little miss grump," Alex whispered in her ear, as she wriggled into place as their very own little spoon, "You have nothing to worry about. I like that you need me. And I need you. Because I am yours as much as you are mine."

She looked over her shoulder, and kissed them then. "I love you."

"I love you too, Tilliebean."

A LONDON LITTLE'S DRAGON

ELLIE ROSE

❧ 12 ❧

Being stranded at the side of the motorway, just outside London, was not fun. In fact, less than not fun, it was downright alarming.

Jamie stood on the hard shoulder and glared at his bike.

For the most part, she ran smoothly but for some reason, it had chosen today of all days to break down.

He crouched down by the fuse box, to see if he could work out what was wrong with her, and tried very fucking hard not to cry.

This was the last thing he needed after this weekend. All he wanted was to get home, jump into bed, and screen cartoons on the projector in his room; and instead, he was stuck at the side of a busy road, on the way back from his ex's wedding.

Jamie wasn't even entirely certain why he'd attended the wedding. The invite had come in the post and all his friends had just assumed that he'd be fine with watching the woman who broke his hear walk down the aisle to the man she'd left him for. And being the people pleaser that he was, he hadn't corrected them. He'd faked happiness and delight, and tried very hard not to flinch when she'd said in the patronising tone—that she knew he hated—that she was proud that he was able to be happy for her.

If anything, he was still pissed off with her: for breaking his heart; for losing him his home; and for ruining Littlespace for him. Cartoons were pretty much all he could cope with sans tears. His stuffies were in a bag at the bottom of his wardrobe, and each time he tried to get one out, he found rogue tears running down his cheeks and he had to put them back.

Luckily, that didn't extend to working on other people's stuffies though, which was just as well considering his job as the mechanics specialist at Stuffie Hospital London.

He looked up from behind his bike as a van pulled up behind him on the hard shoulder, and a woman in a leather jacket jumped out.

"Hey, you okay there?"

Her voice was like butter; soft and warm, and it made him feel prickly in return, all hackles up. Soft, buttery voices made him think of soft Dommes with kind hearts and strong hands, and the ability to stomp his heart into itty bitty pieces. He took a deep breath before he could throw a sarcastic comment her way. It wasn't her fault his ex had hurt him, and he wasn't going to be a dick and take it out on her.

"I think one of her fuses has blown."

"Ah fuck," the woman ran her hand through her hair. "I don't think I've any spares on me, but I own a garage in Peckham, so I can give you a lift and fix it there, if that would help?"

"I mean, are you sure?"

She grinned. "Definitely. It's an easy enough fix, and I'll only charge you for the work, rather than a breakdown service that would turn up here in Gods know how many hours and cost the earth. I'd take a photo of your driver's license and send it to my business partner before I let you in my van though."

"Of course! That would be amazing; thank you so much." To Jamie's horror, he felt a rogue tear escape down his cheek. He dashed the back of his hand across his eyes and tried to gruffly cover it. "I'm sorry; it's been a long weekend."

"Looks it." She strode over and offered him a hand up. "I'm Marian, and I'm a pretty good listener, if you wanna talk about it on the way to the garage."

He met cool grey eyes that should have felt cold, but there was something in them that loosened another tear and he cleared his throat hurriedly. "Yeah, maybe. I'm Jamie."

"Well, Jamie, let's get your bike in the back of my van, and we'll get moving."

Luckily, there was plenty of space in the back of her van, and she had hard points on the side that allowed her secure Jamie's bike so it wouldn't wobble or fall about.

"Just got back from dropping off a BSA Firebird that I restored," she explained. "Hence the space in the van."

There was something, just a little something, that stirred in Jamie's chest. Marian seemed kind, funny, and she repaired and restored motorbikes for a living.

He snuck a look at her as she strode to the van's cab and climbed in. She walked with confidence, no hesitancy whatsoever. It felt oddly reassuring.

He, however, was awkward as all hell, getting all tangled in the seatbelt when he got into the cab, until she took it and did it up with a quirked eyebrow that threatened to undo him.

When they rejoined the motorway, they sat in silence at first. Jamie didn't quite know why it felt so awkward. Perhaps it was the fact that after such a long and difficult weekend he'd had to be rescued, and the last person to rescue him from a difficult situation had been his ex, and look how that had turned out.

But as much as he wanted to hold himself back, there was something that told him that Marion was safe.

"So," she said, breaking the silence. "How did you end up there?"

And all of a sudden, despite the fact that he'd only just met her and that he really did know nothing about her, Jamie found himself telling Marian all about it.

Well, perhaps not quite everything. He wasn't quite ready to explain exactly what the dynamic of his relationship with his ex had been.

The last thing he wanted was for this lovely woman, this lovely, cool, gorgeous woman, to look at him in disgust or confusion. He wanted her to like him, and his previous experiences had implied that most women weren't interested in a guy who wanted to call them Mommy.

But he told her about how he'd fallen in love, and moved in with her, only to have her kick him out when she found someone new.

Marian swore at that. "That wasn't very nice of her."

And for some reason, even though Jamie knew that he agreed with her, he found himself defending his ex. "Well, it was her place first, and I didn't really want to sleep in the living room and hear them having sex next door."

The look she shot him, a momentary flicker of her gaze off the road and onto him, said that he wasn't convincing anyone.

"It was shit," he admitted. "We broke up and I had to find somewhere new to live. If it hadn't been for work…"

"Work?"

He blushed then. "I've never been great at saving money," he admitted. "I'm too impetuous, and end up spending it almost as fast as I earn it. But when work found out what had happened, they loaned me the money for a deposit, and only took it back in small increments over the following year. And one of my colleagues, Daniel, insisted on being my guarantor for the apartment I found."

Jamie smiled at the memory. There were a couple of other Littles at Stuffie Hospital London, but Daniel definitely gave off Caretaker vibes. And even though he'd been embarrassed at the situation, everyone had been so so lovely. Tillie and Alex, who had been inseparable then, and were even more inseparable now that they were dating, had helped him move, and spent the entire weekend coming up with more and more inventive ways for him to layout his furniture.

"Where is it you work?"

"I'm a mechanics specialist at Stuffie Hospital London. We repair old bears and cuddly toys, and give them a new lease of life." He felt himself enthuse and ducked his head, embarrassment washing over him again. "I love my job."

He could hear the smile in Marian's voice. "I can tell; and besides, what Little wouldn't love working with stuffies?"

Her words shocked Jamie into sitting up straight and looking directly at her for the first time since he got into the cab. "I...I..." He could feel his pulse skyrocketing, and his breathing quickened, even as he fought to get it under control. "I mean, I don't know what you, what even is—"

Marian's hand moved from the gearstick to hovering above his knee, as if she wanted to squeeze it reassuringly, and then moved back. "I'm sorry, I just... I know Stuffie Hospital—I went to school with Susie—and I just assumed." She tucked her hair behind her ear, and he realised that she was nervous too. "That wasn't okay. I'm really sorry."

Swallowing once, twice, he shook his head to clear his mind, and then said quietly. "I mean, you're not wrong. I just didn't think that people would be able to guess like that."

She nodded towards his helmet, where a family of

cartoon dogs peeked out from the inside. He'd forgotten about that sticker.

"Oh."

"It's okay," that buttery voice was reassuring now. "I get it."

"You get it." Jamie didn't believe that for a moment. "You know what it's like to be vulnerable and share your innermost childish dreams and hopes, the way a Little does."

Marian paused, and then nodded. "I had a Daddy Dom for a while."

Huh. He hadn't expected that. "Do you have one now?"

The laugh she let out was almost a bark. She sounded more bitter than amused. "No, I don't have a Daddy Dom anymore. Mine wasn't…my Little didn't quite recover from that."

Impetuously, he reached out and touched her shoulder. "That's terrible; I'm so sorry."

Her smile was wistful. "It's okay; my journey took me in a different direction instead. Made me realise that rather than wanting a Caretaker of my own, I'd rather be someone else's Caretaker, and make sure that they never go through what I went through."

"But how do you…? I mean, are you a switch?"

He watched the curve of her neck as she leaned to look behind her before taking a left onto the junction.

"Not really. I mean, I think I probably was once, but these days subbing doesn't really hold any interest for me. I've processed what I went through, made my own safe spaces. Now I want to be able to create and hold a safe space for other people." She paused, and then looked at him as they waited at a set of traffic lights. "How about you? What is it that you want?"

Jamie didn't even hesitate.

"A safe space."

$\maltese$ 13 $\maltese$

Marian's garage was not too far-off Peckham High Street, and as the van pulled in, Jamie found himself wriggling in his seat.

They'd listened to music for much of the rest of the journey, each of them occasionally sneaking glances at the other one, and when they arrived, he found that he was pretty conflicted about their time together coming to an end.

"The garage isn't technically open now," said Marian. "Considering the time." It was gone nine. "I can open it up and sort your fuse now, or if you wanted, you could crash at mine and I'll get it sorted for you tomorrow morning, before you have to get to work."

She looked at him directly, not shying away from the invitation she was making.

"Crash at yours?"

Her grin, when it came, poleaxed him. It spread across her face like a slow sunrise, until her features were lit up with joy. "I'm blunt, it's the autism. I'm saying that I'd like to sleep with you, if you're interested."

That flustered him and he didn't know where to look. "I mean…"

"It's also totally okay if you don't want to; and if you don't feel comfortable waiting for me to sort your bike, you can train it home now, and come pick it up after work instead."

"I'm interested." His words were quiet, but sure.

It made her smile widen and he realised that he might actually do just about anything to see her smile like that. "How about you come up, I throw together some food for us both, and we can talk about what we'd like to do whilst we eat?"

Jamie nodded. "That sounds like a plan."

She lived in the apartment above the garage, in typical crowded London style, and he loved the fact that her place felt light and airy. There were bits of metal and machinery decorating the walls, and he liked the fact that she'd found art that echoed her love for cars and bikes.

There was one particularly fascinating piece that he stood in front of for about fifteen minutes, until she came and stood next to him.

"It's beautiful," he said, because it was. Somehow it took everything that made up a bike, and made it fly. Even static on the wall, it seemed as if it were flying.

"It's the thing I love about bikes," Marian said. "The fact that they make you feel so alive."

He nodded.

"What do you fancy for dinner? I can do some chilli udon noodles. You veggie?"

He shook his head.

"And you're good with spice?"

He nodded.

She laughed, the sound filling the space. "We gotta get you talking more."

"I can talk," he protested, but his laugh intermingled with hers as she took his hand and led him to the couch to sit.

"You sit there whilst I prep."

Watching her cook was mesmerising. She moved from fridge to counter to cupboard to oven without a moment of slowing down. It was like a dance—a marriage of woman and food—and he could see that she adored cooking.

She talked as she cooked, a never-ending river of words bubbling along as she chopped and mixed and wielded her wok.

As she finished, she beckoned him over to lay the table for the two of them, and when she brought the bowls over for them, she said "Good boy," and he thought he might expire.

The food was delicious—spicy and flavourful—and there was momentary silence whilst they ate. Momentary, because after a few minutes, Jamie ventured a question. "Do you have an idea of what you'd like to do this evening?"

She nodded, her eyes flicking to his and then away again. "I'd like to create and hold a safe space for you. What we do within that space is up to you and—" she added before he could interrupt, "I mean it when I say it's what I like most. I get off on knowing that I can help someone get to their happy place. So where's your happy place? What do you like to do there?"

Jamie thought about it for a few moments. "I'm not entirely sure," he admitted. "I mean, I know some of the things I've enjoyed in the past, and I know what I'd *like* to try, but I've never managed to stay in my happy place for very long." The sigh he released sounded sad, even to him, and he took a bite out of a big chunk of broccoli to disguise it. Only the broccoli had been soaked in chilli sauce and he ended up almost spluttering all over the table.

Marian chuckled as she passed him some water. "You okay there?"

He nodded, coughing hoarsely. "Yeah."

"Well, why don't we start with the basics: are you subby?"

Jamie had never had a reputation for being a brat, but the look he shot her definitely had a bratty undertone.

She laughed. "Okay, definitely subby. Do you have a preference for what you'd like to call a Domme?"

Mumbling his reply earned him a tut and a shake of the head.

"Come on, use your words properly please."

"Mommy."

Softness rolled over her face like clouds across a spring sky. "I thought that might be the case. Good boy for telling me." She reached over and patted his hand.

"And if you can imagine your perfect happy place, where would that be?"

"I get a bit overwhelmed sometimes," he said, shy words spilling hesitantly from his lips. "So sometimes being blindfolded helps keep me in the moment. And I like making my Domme come."

Her gurgle of laughter was addictive. He wanted to hear it again.

"And how about orgasms for you?"

Tripping over the words, he explained, "It's not that I don't like orgasms, of course I do, but I'd rather teeter on the edge and let that feeling last for ever. As long as I can please you."

"Oh my sweet boy," she leaned forward and took his face in her hands. "You'll please me." And then she kissed him and everything that had been buzzing around in his head for days, weeks, months, all went silent.

Everything was her. The scent of her hair, her softness, the scratch of her nails as she ran her hands through his short hair.

When she pulled away, he followed her lips, almost keening, desperate for another taste.

"Glass of milk first, and we both wash our hands," she said. "I'm not risking chilli on your tongue."

That made him laugh, and then they were kissing again, moving backwards until she was against the frame of the door. She pulled back, breathless. "Come on, be a good boy for Mommy and have your milk before bed." And then she pulled her top up and over her head.

Damn, he was hard.

She was all soft curves, bountiful breasts threatening to spill out of her bra, and he longed to trace their outline with his tongue. But she leaned back, raised one eyebrow and he found himself pattering over to the fridge, saying "Yes Mommy," like a good boy should.

Jamie could feel her eyes on him as he drank the glass of milk. He wanted to gulp it down, but instead he slowly turned on the spot and looked at her over the rim of the glass.

When he was done, he turned to put it on the counter behind him, and when he turned back, he could see Marian walking into her bedroom, stripping as she went.

As each item of clothing hit the floor, his cock hardened, and his balls tightened up under him, until she was stood there in just her bra.

She was a goddess, and he had every intention of worshipping her.

Jamie followed her, and followed each and every instruction she gave him.

"Jeans off."

"Shirt off."

"On the bed."

"Lie back."

And each time, his obedience was rewarded with a smile and a "good boy".

Finally, when he was lying in front of her, she said, "Safewords?"

"Traffic lights please, Mommy."

"Red for?"

"Stop."

"Yellow for?"

"Pause and check in."

"And green for?"

"Go go go."

She straddled him then, the heat between her legs rubbing against where his cock strained in his boxers. It was all he could do not to haul her into his arms and kiss her.

Clearly, she clocked this, because she asked for his hands, and he gave them to her instantly.

"I think I'd like to tie you up, boy. How do you feel about that?"

His cock twitched and then there was that gurgle of laughter again.

"As much as I'd like to take that as agreement, I think I need a bit more than just your cock saying yes. What do you say?"

"Yes please, Mommy."

Her eyes darkened with desire then, and she swallowed. "Damn if you're not the most darling thing. Okay sweet boy; cuffs or rope?"

"Rope please, Mommy?" And when that sweet sound of rope sliding between fingers arose, he closed his eyes and let his head fall back so he could take it in.

She didn't tie him up immediately, but rather teased him with the rope, running it back and forth across his wrists, his chest, his cheeks, until she deftly caught his left hand and trussed it up. His right hand followed until they were both caught against the headboard, and he could barely move them at all.

Marian ran her finger between the rope and the wrist, testing how tight it was tied, and when he opened his eyes momentarily, her look of satisfaction almost did him in.

"Right. Now for a blindfold I think."

Reaching across him, her bra brushing his face, he felt a soft sound and then a scarf covered his eyes.

Leaning back, he let himself fall into the darkness. Let it swallow him up. Something silky danced across his face, and he realised that it must be her hair, spilling over him.

"Mommy."

"Yes, baby boy?"

He paused. His instinct had been to say 'I love you', but he knew that that wasn't right, that it was too soon. But still, he felt…

"Are you okay, Jamie?"

"Yes, Mommy. Just, you will look after me, won't you?" He could hear the anxiety in his words, worried that it was too much, too demanding.

"Oh darling." She leaned forward until he could feel her lips ghosting his. "I will always look after you. You are precious and you are mine." And then she nudged his head backward and moved up the bed until he was dizzy with the scent of her above him.

"Would you like to lick me, darling boy?"

"Yes, Mommy."

"Beg me."

It was as if her words had unstoppered a waterfall of his own. "Please Mommy, oh Gods, please please please may I lick you. I'm dying to taste you. Desperate to taste you. *Need* to taste you." And he was still talking as she lowered her pussy onto his lips.

He felt like he was drowning in her, alternating between

licking and sucking her clit, using his nose to nudge against it when she shifted so his tongue could enter her.

She tasted divine. Like the finest nectar of the Gods.

And just as with that, he felt like he was drunk on her.

He worshipped.

And she took his worship as her due, riding his face, taking her pleasure from his mouth and tongue as tribute.

Her fingers intertwined with his, tied above his head, and he thought he might come, just like this, just from having her enjoying herself like this, touching him like this.

And when she came, he thought he might expire, thighs tightening, trembling about his ears as she gasped out her pleasure in a different key.

She wasn't done with him though. Straddling his waist, pussy perfectly nestled atop his cock, despite the layer of cotton between them, she took off the blindfold and he came blinking into the light.

"Hey there, darling boy," she said. Her hair was all mussed up, ginger waves riotously curling about her, and her lips were pink and full and he longed to kiss them. "You made Mommy very very happy."

"I did?"

Her throaty chuckle asserted that yes, she had had a most excellent time indeed. "So much so, my good boy, that I think you deserve a reward." And then she leaned behind her and in one swift movement, undid the clasp of her bra.

Her breasts were heavy and rounded and he felt himself struggle to try and sit up, but she hushed him and pushed him back down. "Now now, darling boy, no fussing."

And then she leaned over him and moaned as her nipple met his lips. "Here you go."

She didn't need to say another word, he sucked the tight nub into his mouth and she gasped. One breast, and then the other, and then back again, he lavished them with attention, sucking and flicking with his tongue, and at one point a tiny nip that had her grinding against his cock.

He thought he might explode any moment, but he loved even more the fact that this wasn't about him, or his pleasure. This was all about her, all about being a good boy for Mommy, and making her feel good.

But when she came a second time, the heat from her pussy scalding his cock through his boxers, her nipple in his mouth, and her hand gently stroking his hair, he followed her over the cliff into bliss.

Afterwards though, he felt almost ashamed of his lack of self-control, and wouldn't look at her when she said his name.

"Jamie. *Jamie.*"

She tapped the side of his face, just to make him turn to look at her, but he gasped and she saw his need in his eyes.

"Say it."

"But, Mommy…"

"*Say it.*"

"I'm a bad boy, Mommy."

"Yes, you are, but you're *my* bad boy. And what happens when my bad boy comes before I tell him to?"

He knew that this was the point where he could back out of it, where he could close off and not tell her what he really wanted, but her eyes were full of kindness and affection and…

"Bad boys get slapped and bad boys get spanked."

❧ 14 ❧

The first slap was gentle, more gentle than he wanted, but when she looked down at him, he said "Green green green, Mommy. Please, Mommy, more." And she nodded at him.

The second one was sharp and took his breath away and had his cock surging back to life with a speed that surprised even him.

He turned his head and kissed the palm that had kissed his cheek.

"Again?"

"Yes please, Mommy."

Then he was biting his lip as the third slap shocked him with its fierceness.

And then she was undoing the rope about his wrists with trembling, eager fingers, and beckoning him forward until he was on all fours beside her.

"Count them off for me, boy, and thank me."

"Yes, Mommy."

The spanks started harder than the slaps had, and soon he was mumbling words and numbers and thank yous in a jumble of sounds that echoed even as his balls bounced and his cock bobbed beneath him.

Each spank felt—just as the slaps had—like a kiss.

Like she knew exactly what he needed.

Like she was giving him the space he needed just to be.

And then her hand was reaching beneath him, pausing just beyond his tip and until he surged forward, desperate to feel her skin against his.

She moved it away and laughed, a laugh that was both mocking and comforting.

"You want this, do you, boy? You want my touch?"

"Please, Mommy." His head was starting to spin now, the high from subspace making his movements slow down and last forever. "Please, Mommy, I need you."

Marian spanked him again, hard. "But you were a bad boy…"

"I'm sorry, Mommy, I'm so sorry, I won't be a bad boy again!"

"You promise?"

"Yes Mommy, I promise," and then her hand was round his length, her thumb sliding across his slick tip, and he buried his face into the pillows and tried beyond tried to keep his orgasm at bay.

It was almost as if she knew exactly what would make him come, because each time she' back off, edging him just a little bit more. Just like he'd asked her to.

"You make such beautiful desperate noises, darling boy," she said. "Mommy's desperate Little boy."

He didn't know how long she edged him for; it could have been minutes, it could have been hours. But when she finally brought him so close he could almost taste the pleasure, she leaned forward, her breasts stroking his back, and said, "Not tonight, there's a good boy."

And he squeezed his eyes closed and took deep breaths

and kept himself right there on the edge, until he could feel the orgasms ebb away into nothingness.

Jamie collapsed on the bed, curling up into a ball, and she took him in her arms and held him.

"You did so so well, my darling boy. I'm so so proud of you."

He lay there trembling in her arms, letting her words sooth his soul.

Marian pulled him close into her, and he felt her legs slide into place next to his, like they were two pieces in Tetris.

"Thank you, Mommy," he whispered, and she kissed his shoulder and held him tight all night.

WHEN HE AWOKE the next morning, she was nowhere to be seen, and for a moment, he thought she'd left for work without waking him, but then she came in with toast cut into dragon shapes, an airtight container, and a dragon stuffie.

Jamie looked at the dragon stuffie, and for the first time in a year, when he picked it up his heart didn't feel like it was breaking. He didn't feel like throwing up. He didn't feel like crying.

He felt happy.

"This is for me?"

Marian smiled at him. "He's been sat waiting for his owner for far too long. I'm glad he gets to be yours," she said, and leaned in to get a kiss.

He beamed up at her, and then wriggled so he could kiss her back. "Morning, Mommy." And he picked up the dragon stuffie, and cuddled it to him, burying his face in its softness.

He had a stuffie. A new stuffie that promised good memories and delight.

"You'd best hurry up and eat; I can probably drop you at

work before the garage opens, and then I can bring your bike by at the end of the day."

He looked at her, wide eyed, and she stopped talking.

"Oh fuck, I just assumed—" she flushed red and he realised that she was embarrassed. "It's fine, I'll speed it up, and then you can go and—"

"—hey." Jamie interrupted her gently. "Rewind a second; did you make me a packed lunch?"

"Yes?" she looked nervous, as if scared that she'd messed up.

"Thank you, Mommy," he said, and this time it was his turn to kiss her. His hands were in her hair and he held her close. "That makes me feel really cared for, and cherished."

"Yes, but I shouldn't have assumed…"

"Shouldn't have assumed what?"

"That you'd want to do this again."

He paused and thought for a moment. "Well, in this case, you would be correct." Jamie ducked his head and blushed. "You said last night that I was yours."

"You are mine." Her words were quiet, but they held a ring of truth that made him smile. "Not in a creepy controlling sense, but in an I've got you kind of sense."

"I think I'm going to like being yours," he said. "Because it feels like love."

She kissed him and touched his cheek affectionately. "Good, because I intend to love you very much."

And holding his dragon in his arms, Jamie believed her. She was his safe space.

ABOUT ELLIE ROSE

Ellie Rose is a queer author who writes fluffy and steamy Little romances. Her books are kinky and neurodiverse, and always have a Happy Ever After!

When she's not writing, she can invariably be found reading in her princess tent, surrounded by a mountain of stuffies, or dancing in a silent disco for one in her living room.

Follow Ellie on Facebook, join her Facebook group The Shenanigans Squad, and sign up to her Newsletter to keep up to date with everything Stuffie Hospital!